Ruffles

and the **new** green thing

David Melling

This is **Ruffles.**

Ruffles **loves** . . .

singing . . .

scratching . . .

eating . . .

fetching . . .

sniffing . . .

chewing . . .

digging . . .

running . . .

and sleeping.

Ruffles **does not love** the new green thing.

And the **new green** thing is sitting in his bowl.

Ruffles has never seen anything like it before.

New. And green. And sitting in his bowl.

What **is** it?

Ruffles thinks . . .   and creeps . . .   and stares . . .

and listens . . .   and circles . . .   and pokes . . .

and sits . . .   and smells . . .   and thinks again.

But look! Ralph has come to play.

Ralph always digs the **deepest** holes . . .

Ralph always finds the **biggest** sticks . . .

And Ralph always jumps the **highest** fences.

And they **both** love to . . .

tug . . .   and scratch . . .   and play . . .

and run . . .   and race . . .   and chase . . .

and howl . . .   and leap . . .   and sleep.

The **new green** thing is still in Ruffles' bowl . . .

Ralph looks at it. And takes a **big** bite.

Gulp!

Well! If Ralph can try the new green thing . . .

then Ruffles can too!

He nibbles . . .   and gnaws . . .   and chews . . .

and munches . . .   and crunches . . .   and chomps . . .

and gobbles . . .   and guzzles . . .   and gulps until . . .

the **new green** thing is **all gone.**

And it was . . .

delicio

us!

Ruffles **loves** . . .

singing . . .

scratching . . .

eating . . .

fetching . . .

sniffing . . .

chewing . . .

digging . . .

running . . .

and Ralph.

But most of all, Ruffles **loves** new things . . .

Unless they're orange.